peg + cat

THE BIG DOG PROBLEM

A LEVEL **2** READER

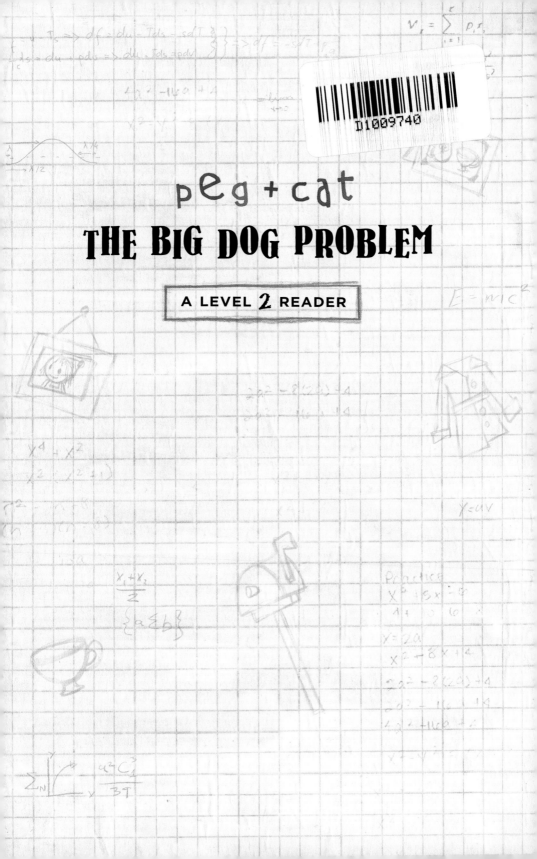

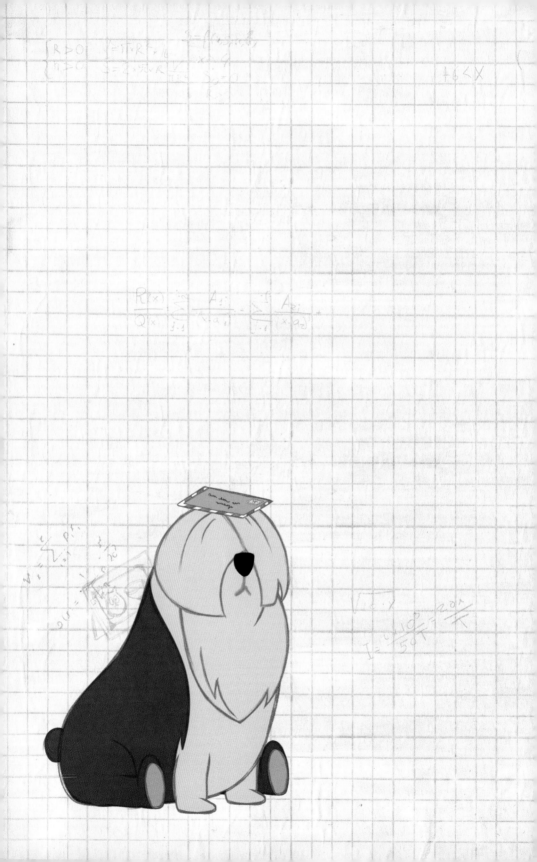

peg + cat

THE BIG DOG PROBLEM

A LEVEL 2 READER

JENNIFER OXLEY
+ BILLY ARONSON

CANDLEWICK
ENTERTAINMENT

This book is based on the TV series *Peg + Cat*.
Peg + Cat is produced by The Fred Rogers Company.
Created by Jennifer Oxley and Billy Aronson.
The Big Dog Problem is based on a television script
by Dustin Ferrer.
Art assets assembled by Sarika Matthew.
The PBS KIDS logo is a registered mark of the Public
Broadcasting Service and is used with permission.

pbskids.org/peg

First edition 2017

Library of Congress Catalog Card Number pending
ISBN 978-0-7636-9787-7 (hardcover)
ISBN 978-0-7636-9790-7 (paperback)

17 18 19 20 21 22 APS 10 9 8 7 6 5 4 3 2 1

Printed in Humen, Dongguan, China

This book was typeset in OPTITypewriter.
The illustrations were created digitally.

Candlewick Entertainment
an imprint of Candlewick Press
99 Dover Street
Somerville, Massachusetts 02144

visit us at www.candlewick.com

Contents

Chapter 1
Really Important Letters

Peg's mom gave her five letters to mail.

Peg showed Cat the letters.

"Four important letters," said Peg. "And one REALLY important red letter. She gave them to us to mail because we're growing up."

Peg showed Cat the height marks on the wall.

"What is height?" asked Cat.

"Height is how tall something is," said Peg.

She drew a new mark above the others.

"Now I am this tall," she said. "You are taller, too."

"We are tall enough to mail letters," said Cat.

"I can hold these three letters. You can hold these two," said Peg.

"Or I can take three and you can take two," said Cat.

4

"I can take four. You can hold one," said Peg.

"I will hold four. You can hold one," said Cat.

"Let's divide the letters up with fair sharing," said Peg.

One for Peg. One for Cat.

One for Peg. One for Cat.

Oh, no! There was an extra letter.

"These letters can't be divided fairly," said Cat.

"We've got a BIG PROBLEM!" said Peg.

Peg handed Cat the extra
letter.

"You can hold it."

Cat passed the letter
back to Peg. "You can have it,"
said Cat.

They passed the letter back
and forth.

That way, they each got to
hold it for the same amount
of time as they walked to the
mailbox.

Peg and Cat sang:
"Problem solved!
The problem is solved!
We solved the problem.
Problem solved!"

Chapter 2
The Very Big Dog

Peg and Cat got to the mailbox.

A very big dog sat in front of it.

"Right now, I do not feel very tall," said Peg.

"Arf!" Big Dog barked.

"Run!" shouted Peg.

Peg and Cat ran back to
Peg's house.

"I am totally afraid of that
dog!" said Peg.

"And we can't get to the
mailbox without going past him,"
said Cat.

"We've got a REALLY BIG PROBLEM!" said Peg. "What should we do?"

"We could sneak behind him," said Cat.

Peg drew a plan.

PLAN #1

"Come and take a look at
this plan. We will sneak up
from behind the dog," said Peg.

Peg and Cat walked behind
the dog. "Go a little faster,
Cat! Move those feet!"

17

"I think he hears us,"
said Cat.

"Retreat!" Peg and Cat
yelled.

Peg drew a new plan.

PLAN #2

"This time, we will go
farther behind the dog,"
said Peg.

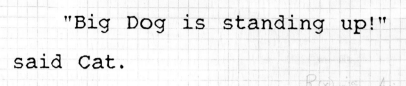

"Big Dog is standing up!"
said Cat.

"Run!" said Peg.

Peg drew a third plan.

"I hope you're feeling
bouncy," she said to Cat.

"Why?" asked Cat.

"Because we will go right
over him. We will bounce really
high," said Peg.

"Big Dog is way too tall!
I don't know what to do," said
Cat.

"Let's go!" said Peg.

"I'm way ahead of you,"
said Cat.

They ran.

Chapter 3
One More Try

Peg drew one last plan.

"This will be a daring stunt," she said. "We'll throw a stick behind the dog. Then we will run in front."

Peg threw the stick.

"Look. Our plan is working! He is going to go and play. Oops! He sees us. Run away!" said Peg.

Peg and Cat ran right into
Peg's mom. They dropped the
letters.

"Did you mail the letters?"
asked Peg's mom.

"No," said Peg.

"Have you been dillydallying?"
asked Peg's mom.

"Maybe a little," said Cat.

"Cat and I are totally going
to mail these letters," said Peg.
She picked up the letters.

"We can't let my mom know
we're scared. She will never
give us another grown-up job,"
said Peg.

"Why aren't grown-ups scared of anything?" asked Cat.

"Maybe because they are really tall," said Peg.

"I wish I were tall," said Cat.

"That's it! You amazing Cat!" Peg ran into the house.

"You will get on my shoulders. I will put on the coat. We will look like a really tall person."

They were ready to face Big Dog.

Chapter 4
Problem Solved

Peg and Cat walked toward
Big Dog.

"He isn't scared of us at
all," said Cat.

"Let's increase our height,"
said Peg. She stood on top of
two sticks.

Big Dog moved closer to
Peg and Cat.

"Run!" they shouted.

The letters! Where were they?

"I got two," said Peg.

"I got two," said Cat.

"Where is the REALLY important letter?" asked Peg.

It was on Big Dog!

"I can't let my mom down," said Peg.

"I'm going in!"

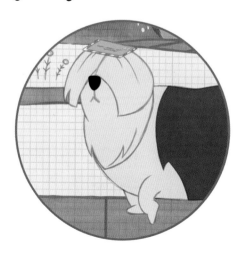

Peg ran up to Big Dog.
She reached for the letter on
his head.

BOOM! She fell down. The letter went flying.

Big Dog came very close to Peg.

"Please don't hurt me, Your Bigness," said Peg.

Big Dog sniffed Peg.

"I will save you!" said Cat.
"Big Dog is helping me up,"
said Peg.

Big Dog licked Peg.
"He is as cuddly as
a kitten!" said Peg.
Big Dog licked
Cat, too.
"You're tickling
me, big guy!"
said Cat.

A truck honked.

"The mail truck!" said Peg.

"Right now, we have to mail
some important letters."

"And one REALLY important
letter," said Cat.
They ran to the mailbox.
Peg could not reach it.

Cat jumped on her head.
But they were still not tall
enough.

"I am TOTALLY FREAKING OUT!"
said Peg.

Cat held up his hands.

"Cat is right. I should count backward from five to calm down," said Peg. "Five, four, three, two, one," she counted.

Big Dog lifted Peg and
Cat up.

"You genius dog! Now we can
reach the mailbox!" said Peg.

"Because we know about height, we are totally mailing four important letters and one REALLY important letter!" said Peg.

"With a little help from a big friend," said Cat.

"We did it!" yelled Peg. "We mailed all five letters!"

Peg and Cat sang:

"Problem solved!

The problem is solved!

We solved the problem!

So everything is awesome!

Problem solved!"